Trouble on the Day

Norma Clarke and Peter Kavanagh

Collins

For Tishian and Louisa

For Kevin, the best page boy ever

Best Friends • Jessy and the Bridesmaid's Dress •
Jessy Runs Away • **Rachel Anderson**
Changing Charlie • Clogpots in Space • **Scoular Anderson**
Ernest the Heroic Lion-tamer • Ivana the Inventor • **Damon Burnard**
Two Hoots • **Helen Cresswell**
Magic Mash • Nina's Machines • **Peter Firmin**
Shadows on the Barn • **Sarah Garland**
Clever Trevor • The Mystery of Lydia Dustbin's Diamonds • Nora Bone •
Nora Bone and the Tooth Fairy • **Brough Girling**
Sharon and Darren • **Nigel Gray**
Thing-in-a-Box • Thing-on-Two-Legs • **Diana Hendry**
Desperate for a Dog • More Dog Trouble • **Rose Impey**
Georgie and the Dragon • Georgie and the Planet Raider • **Julia Jarman**
Cowardy Cowardy Cutlass • Cutlass Rules the Waves • Free With Every Pack •
Mo and the Mummy Case • The Fizziness Business • **Robin Kingsland**
And Pigs Might Fly! • Albertine, Goose Queen • Jigger's Day Off •
Martians at Mudpuddle Farm • Mossop's Last Chance •
Mum's the Word • **Michael Morpurgo**
Granny Grimm's Gruesome Glasses • **Jenny Nimmo**
Grubble Trouble • **Hilda Offen**
Hiccup Harry • Harry Moves House • Harry's Party • Harry the Superhero •
Harry with Spots On • **Chris Powling**
Grandad's Concrete Garden • **Shoo Rayner**
Rattle and Hum – Robot Detectives • **Frank Rodgers**
Our Toilet's Haunted • **John Talbot**
Pesters of the West • **Lisa Taylor**
Lost Property • **Pat Thomson**
Monty the Dog Who Wears Glasses • Monty Bites Back • Monty Ahoy! •
Monty Must Be Magic! • Monty – Up To His Neck in Trouble! • **Colin West**
Ging Gang Goolie, It's an Alien • **Bob Wilson**

First published in Great Britain by
A & C Black (Publishers) Ltd 1995
First published by Collins 1996

Collins is an imprint of HarperCollins Children's Books part of
HarperCollins Publishers Ltd. 77-85 Fulham Palace Road, London W6 8JB

Text copyright © Norma Clarke 1995.
Illustrations copyright © Peter Javanagh 1995

ISBN 978-0-00-675102-1

CHAPTER ONE

The way it started was like this.
I always wake up early.
My eczema wakes me.
And this morning
I woke up even
earlier than usual.

There was a
pale light coming
through the curtains.
I scratched where I was itching
— fingers, big toe, knees. Then I
leaned over and shook my brother Robin.

Robin loves sleeping. I shook him again.
Robin's not much use as a brother but
he's the only one I've got.

Robin said, 'Gerroff. Go away.' Then,

Robin likes chasing baddies.

'Not baddies,' I said. I didn't want him getting up, I only wanted him awake. It's boring when you're awake on your own.

'Think of a long word,' I said. I can say any long word backwards. I practise when I'm lying in bed.

But Robin was gone. I heard him clumping down the stairs. Then I heard him come back again, running.

It was a stupid game, but I put on my specs, shuffled into my slippers and followed Robin downstairs. The front door was wide open.

Did you open that?

I told you. It's the baddies. They've gone to get reinforcements. Quick. Let's chase after them.

I caught Robin by his collar. It was lucky I was there to stop him.

6

We listened. Out of the front door you could see the doorstep, the path, a bit of a wall on one side and a bit of hedge on the other. The street was quiet, grey and very still. The gate was gently swinging.

I heard a sound like somebody closing the back door of a van.

Robin twisted out from under me, ran down the path and out through the open gate. I followed him.

I was just in time to see a light-blue van drive the wrong way down our one-way street.

8

I tried. DML something. But I did get
a good look at the driver. A big man
with a fat, frowning face.

9

I would have said something if it wasn't
for what happened next.

'Tom!' I turned round and there was
my mum, standing in the front doorway
in her nightdress and bare feet.
Looking annoyed.

Do you know what time it is?
Some people are trying to sleep.

CHAPTER TWO

Robin! You're in your bare feet. You'll catch your death!

We were bundled inside and shooed into
the kitchen. No chance to think or explain.
All my family's like that except me.
Rush, rush. Do this. Do that. And they
all talk a lot. I couldn't get a word in.
Mum said, 'This morning of all mornings,
when I've got so much on my mind.'
She looked out of the kitchen window.
'Still, at least they're going to have
a nice day for it.'

'What?' I said, and then I remembered.

It was the wedding. Mum's sister, Tina, was getting married. And Robin and I had to stand behind her, and I had to hold her long dress off the ground when she walked into the church.

Me. Tom Bold. Nine years and nine months old exactly. Everybody watching, including toffee-nosed cousin Harriet and her horrible Dad, my Uncle Charlie.
I felt sick.

'You boys are going to look lovely,' Mum said. 'Just lovely.'

There were two hangers on the back of the door. There were two frilly purple satin shirts hanging on the hangers.

'I'm not wearing one of those shirts,' I said.

'Don't be difficult,' Mum said. We'd had this row already, if you can call it a row. I'd said, 'I won't.' Mum had said, 'You will, I'm in no mood to be argued with.'

She wasn't in a mood to be argued with now, either.

'And these are the shoes,' she said, taking them out of a box. They were shiny black, with silver buckles.

I'm not wearing them.

And these are the trousers. Aren't they adorable?

She held up a pair of velvet shorts.

'I won't,' I said.

'And these . . .'
She fished about in a plastic bag.
'These are the tights.'
She held them up.
White.

'Darling,' Mum said.
'It's what Auntie Tina wants,
and today's her special day.'

Two things happened then. First the
phone rang, which Robin ran to get.
It was Gran, checking we were awake
and had remembered what day it was.

15

Second, Dad came into the kitchen
looking sleepy and puzzled.

Who took the new sound system out of the living room? I spent all evening setting it up. And why are your computer games all over the floor?

BADDIES!

BURGLARS!

Robin dropped the phone and dashed down the passage to the sitting room. He was always quicker than me.

Robin was on his knees searching like a
madman through the mess.
'My Gameboy!' he shrieked.
'Where's my Gameboy?'

They took my
Gameboy!

Mum hugged us both tightly.

Dad said, 'They must have come in through the window and walked out through the front door. Cheek!'
He looked around to see if anything else had gone. Only the sound system was missing.

'And my Gameboy,' Robin sniffed.

19

You were right about the baddies.

I said to Robin to cheer him up.

Of all the mornings they had to choose!

She needed cheering up too.

Isn't it a pity we can't go to the wedding after all?

Oh yes we can! And we'll have a jolly good time, burglars or no burglars!

Mum wasn't the sort to let a little thing like burglars upset her plans.

20

Dad said, 'I'll stay and deal with the police.'

'I'll ring 999!' Robin cried, leaping out of Mum's arms.

Dad caught him.

It took two of them to get Robin upstairs. I went quietly.
Everybody in our family is big and bossy.
I'm different. I'm small and cunning.

When
it was my
turn, I stayed
under the shower
a long time, trying to
think up a
cunning way
to catch the
burglars
and get out
of being a
page-boy
wearing   stupid
                               clothes
                               and being
                               laughed at
                               by my
                               cousin
                               Harriet.
                               But I
                               couldn't.

I got out of the shower and dried myself.
In the bedroom, I saw Robin. He had
already been dressed.

CHAPTER THREE

Gran was the first person we saw when we arrived at the church for the wedding. There were crowds of people standing about. Gran burst from the mob and pulled open our car door.

She came and gave me and Robin a big hug.

Gran pressed toffees into our hands.

Tina's boyfriend, Lee, who's a stunt man in the films, had broken his ankle jumping off a four-storey building. He was on crutches, waiting to get married. He didn't look very happy.

Tina arrived inside a horse-drawn carriage. She didn't look like Tina at all.

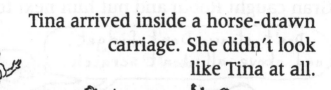

She looked
like a snow-capped
mountain on the move.
Lee disappeared into the church.
Robin ran after him, but Lee still won.

I stood behind Tina and held up her train. 'Is Lee in there?' she said. 'Have they got the ring?'

Gran caught Robin and put him next to me.

Don't stray. Don't fidget, and above all don't scratch.

Lee's going to America. He's going to parachute into the Grand Canyon.

Don't any of you try and do what he does for a living when you grow up. It's a stupid job.

They got burgled this morning. Today of all days!

My Gameboy. I was going to play my Gameboy. What am I going to do if I get bored?

'Hold these,' said Gran, shoving a bunch of flowers into his fist.

I wondered if our house would be all right when we got home.

We started slow-walking forward.

'Mind where you put your big feet,' Gran said to all of us, giving Grandad a special look. Tina's white dress spread out everywhere like a fan.

It was crowded inside the church, and hot.
People stared at us. I had a job keeping
Tina's dress off the ground. Robin was
no use. He had the flowers in his hands
and he was busy picking the petals off
one by one.

'I'm hungry,' he whispered to me.

Mum spotted us and waved and smiled.
Gran was sitting beside her. I had to stare.
Gran – our Gran – was dabbing her eyes
with a little hankie.

When we got to the front we stopped.
I arranged Tina's dress so we didn't trip
on it.

The music suddenly ended and people
coughed and cleared their throats.

I looked around. Rows and rows of people stood waiting. Then a baby screamed.

My legs ached. My fingers and the back of my knees itched. My toe itched, too. I put my other foot on it and pressed but it's hard to scratch through a shoe.

I imagined being able to take the shoe off and scratch and scratch. I tried thinking up words backwards. I said my name a few times. Dlob Mot. And Robin's – Dlob Nibor. Tina was an edirb. Lee was a moorgedirb. I was a yob egap.

At last we started walking again. We crowded into a little room.

'Wait till you see what we've got laid out in the buffet tent,' Tina told Robin. 'And then there's a band coming, and we're all going to dance . . .'

'Especially me,' Lee said, waving his crutch.

'Tom and Robin will show us the new dances,' Tina said gaily as we lined up to parade back down the aisle and out of the church.

CHAPTER FOUR

Of all the big and bossy people in our family, Uncle Charlie is the worst.

Ha. Ha. Ha.

'Well Tom, have you grown since I last saw you? Stand up. Let's have a look at you.'

I wished I was six feet tall, and that the ground would open up and swallow Uncle Charlie whole.

'Your problem is, you don't eat,' Uncle Charlie boomed on. It certainly wasn't *his* problem. 'I bet you haven't been to the buffet tent yet.'

'No,' piped up Robin. 'We're just going.'

'This way,' Uncle Charlie said, and pushed me inside.

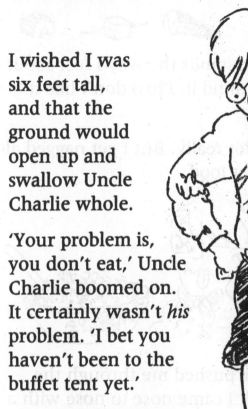

Nobody understands the way I feel about food. I don't mind it, I just don't like it messed about.

I eat quite a lot really. But I get nagged all the time about food.

Uncle Charlie pushed me through the buffet tent till I came nose to nose with a bowl of slimy spaghetti twirls all mixed up with green pepper and other green, red and black bits and things.

'Here,' he said, handing me a plate and taking one for himself.
'What a marvellous spread!'

I took the plate. This was worse than being burgled. This was worse than being dressed like someone in a pantomime. It was worse than anything.

36

Here. You'll like this.

Uncle Charlie slopped a slab of cold white chicken with yellow sauce on my plate. Then he spooned a splodge of something greeny-grey all over it. I tipped the plate and it slid about.

Avocado mousse. My favourite!

'Uncle Charlie . . .' I said, swallowing hard. 'I can't eat this.'

'Yes you can,' he said. 'You need building up. It's no good being fussy about food.'

He pulled a bowl of evil-looking mushrooms towards him.

'Mushrooms make me ill!' I shrieked. 'Ask my mum. She'll tell you!'

Where was my mum? I looked around for her desperately. Where was Robin?

Luckily, I saw Tina and Lee. Luckily, Uncle Charlie saw them too. They were standing at the other end of the table, Lee balancing on his crutches, and they were looking worried and miserable.

We've been let down by the band. They've just sent a message to say they're not coming. They've had a row and decided to part for ever.

'Not coming?' said Uncle Charlie.

Gran heard and she came over.
'What's this? Not coming? I knew it!'

Mum said, 'We can't have a party without a band.'

Leave this to me!

I threw my plate under the table.

CHAPTER FIVE

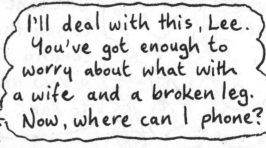

I'll deal with this, Lee. You've got enough to worry about what with a wife and a broken leg. Now, where can I phone?

Gran had a mobile phone in her handbag.

I know a man who knows a man. Best DJ in the business. You don't need a band. He'll have everyone up and dancing. Even Lee. Ha, ha, ha!

He put the phone to his ear. After a bit, he shook his head and pressed some other numbers. He shook the phone.

Your battery must be flat.

There's nothing wrong with MY battery!

Gran showed him
the On/Off switch.
'Mine's a different
model,' Uncle
Charlie said, puffing.

'Right,' he said, after talking loudly for
some time. 'That's sorted that out. I've
got him for you. It wasn't easy. He's been
a bit busy but he's coming over right
away, as a favour.'

He gave Gran back her phone, looking
pleased with himself.

'Are you sure?'
Tina looked worried.
'I mean, do you
know this man?
Have you seen
him working?'

Uncle Charlie pecked
her on the cheek.

Trust me.

Uncle Charlie went out to watch for the
DJ and show him where to put his gear.

When Harriet came up, I slipped away.
But she followed me.

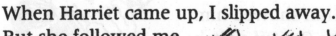

Don't tell me they're letting Dad take charge? They must need their brains tested.

We prowled round the outside of the buffet tent. She didn't mention ponies once. And she didn't say anything about the wedding. She was almost normal.

Robin was sitting on the church wall and Uncle Charlie was pacing up and down on the pavement outside.

But how do we know if he's any good, Uncle Charlie?

Why don't you run along and get yourself a lemonade, Robin? Leave me to handle this.

There was a big tree with low spreading branches in the churchyard. Harriet was good at climbing trees, so we climbed up high and sat there hidden. Harriet said

Think of a number. Double it. Add any number.

Hang on...

Halve it.

Wait a minute...

Take away the number you first thought of.

What number?

Before I could work it out, I heard Robin. He was running towards the buffet tent, yelling my name.

CHAPTER SIX

'It's a pale blue van!' Robin said.
'It's the same one.'

Uncle Charlie was standing outside the buffet tent, holding people back while a skinny man with a pointed black beard carried some gear through.

It's the other burglar.

Don't be stupid.

He must be a baddie. It's the same van.

No it's not.

It is. You haven't even come to see it.

No but I did see the burglar before and he didn't look like that man.

Oh shut up, you two. You're so boring.

I followed Harriet into the tent. A small stage had been fitted up and there were boxes and loudspeakers and lights. Standing on the stage, fiddling with the equipment, was a big man I had seen before. A man with a fat, frowning face.

CHAPTER SEVEN

Now I needed to be cunning. But first I needed to be absolutely sure they were our burglars. I slipped away from Harriet and ran down the path out of the churchyard. I found Robin crouching behind the church wall.

He's inside the van. He's been there ages.

The van door closed with a thud. I ducked down beside Robin. Something was going

THUMP 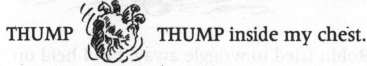 THUMP inside my chest.

The skinny man walked by. He didn't see us. He was carrying a box with *Golden Oldies* written in gold letters on the side.

'Come on,' Robin said, as soon as the skinny man was out of sight.

We walked all round the van. It was pale blue, scratched in places. The licence number was DML 565D.

Robin tried to wriggle away, but I held on tight. I may be small, but I'm surprisingly strong. People are always surprised at how strong I am.

We were struggling our way round the van, when I noticed something. 'Robin,' I said, letting go. 'What's that on the dashboard?'

He jumped up on the bonnet to get a better look through the windscreen.

Dad appeared, hurrying towards the church.

'Dad!' I cried.

He said, 'Robin! What are you doing? Get down off there!'

Robin said, 'We found the burglars! Look! And they've been playing with my Gameboy! Cheek!'

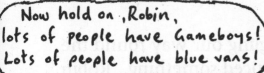

We looked. Sure enough, there were tiny white spots all over the Gameboy.

'It's still not enough proof,' Dad said. 'And we don't want to spoil the wedding party.'

We could hear some old-fashioned dance music and people laughing.

We chased after Robin.

They were the burglars and no mistake.
Hastily, they tried to pack up their gear
and run away.

Lee was too quick for them. He tripped up the skinny one with his plaster cast

and pinned the big one down with a crutch. Tina sat on him.

Uncle Charlie just stood there like a whale with his mouth opening and shutting. I took Gran's mobile phone from him. I dialled 999.

CHAPTER EIGHT

'It's all stolen,' the policeman said, unplugging the equipment. 'We'll have to take it away.'

WHAT ABOUT OUR PARTY!

Robin tugged at Dad's arm. 'I still haven't got my Gameboy out of the van.'

'Hang on, Robin,' Dad said impatiently.

I followed Robin down to the van where another policeman was busy sorting through stuff. I stood and watched, wondering if I would ever grow tall enough to be a policeman. Robin snatched his Gameboy off the dashboard and ran away.

57

The policeman showed me something that had been wedged in a dark corner of the van and covered with a plastic sheet.

It was our stereo that had been stolen.

All the stolen equipment had been taken out of the tent. Only the stage was left and some special sockets for plugging in a sound system.

The policeman helped us set up our own system after we carried it carefully out of the van.

It's new actually.

And it hasn't been damaged. It should be a jolly good sound.

All the people who lived near enough went home to collect their favourite music.

How about some reggae?

Techno!

Rock n' roll!

Let's have some jazz!

'Pitiful, isn't it?' Harriet said, as Tina and Lee made a special request for something called *Love Me Do*.

I felt shy all of a sudden,
especially with Harriet watching.

'I bet Harriet knows some dances,' said
Tina.

'Me? I can't dance to this,' Harriet said,
offended.

Tina put her hands on her hips. 'Who am I going to dance with? Lee's no use. I've got to dance with somebody.'

'No use?' Lee hopped over on one crutch.

Stand aside!

'Well,' Mum said to Gran. 'What an amazing coincidence, catching the burglars and getting our sound system back like that.'

They were standing at the edge of the dance circle, watching. 'Coincidence? Rubbish,' said Gran. 'Smart boys you've got, especially Tom. He's a thinker, that one. I couldn't have done better myself.'

Gran came and joined the dance. Mum started dancing, Uncle Charlie joined, even Harriet let herself be pulled in.

Robin sat in a corner playing with his Gameboy. Dad worked the sound system and kept the music going.

We danced all the dances we knew. We twirled and swung and bumped into each other. Tina taught me to jive. Harriet showed us how to dance hip-hop. Mum and Dad bopped and Uncle Charlie did the twist. Everybody was happy. Gran laughed so much she cried. It was the best wedding rave ever . . .